MEETING A ZOMBIE

UNNATI BHARDWAJ

To my mother, her love and mystery!

Contents

Prologue

'What is your new project which is not letting you sleep, daddy?' Manny asked his dad, Vanshul who was still engrossed in the computer screen.

'We are researching a virus. A special virus. Now only the analytical conclusion has to be given. We are determining the potential of this virus, whether it can kill zombies or not.' Vanshul replied.

'What is a zombie?' the little kid asked eagerly.

'A human killer or eater.'

'Have you met one?'

'Never. They haven't still invaded our planet but they may, in anytime soon. Nevertheless, we'll be safe by then. Our project is planned in such a way,' Vanshul replied proudly.

'But I want to. I want to meet a human eater. I will reveal all your nefarious plans to him, about how you've planned to kill him,' Manny giggled.

Vanshul laughed back.

'If you had researched on Manny`s disease, he would have been eligible to go to school. What you're doing lately is a waste of time and nothing else,' Anubhuti said impudently.

'It is not easy to find or rather create other lives, you must know that I am not God, Anubhuti,' Vanshul replied annoyingly.

'Come, beta. Don't waste your time on futile things. Your father is so selfish that he doesn't want to even think of the things existing around him.' Then she reached out for a spoon to feed her son.

Manny had figured out that his parents were upset with each other but there was hardly a thing that he could perform, for he was small and also because he had not understood the foremost cause of their stressed minds.

ONE

It was a stormy February morning. The sun had not shown up in the sky, making the weather terrible. During winters, we crave the sunshine and the sun craves to see us craving.

Anubhuti was serving breakfast to her husband.

'The food tastes good,' Vanshul commented while taking the second bite.

Anubhuti remained quiet.

'You're looking beautiful in this yellow cardigan,' he said and looked up at her for an answer.

She shook her head. 'Vanshul, I'm not upset with you,' she continued, 'I'm just worried for

Manny. We live in a world where without education, you can survive but cannot thrive. Schooling is the foundation of life values, knowledge, discipline, and learning. He's ten now and has yet never gone to school. His future frights me. Don't you want him to be successful?'

Vanshul stood up and took her hands into his.

'Calm down, beautiful lady. Comprehend him. He is a distinctive kid. He's like a seedling that needs special care together with attention and with that it turns out to be a precious shady tree bearing flowers and berries. More than his academics, I'm concerned for his health. Once he gets alright, I will make sure to make him one of the ablest men of all times.'

'I pray the same. Hope the same happens,' she replied not being very pleased with his answer.

'What about sending Manny to a school in a week?' he asked, noticing his wife's obnoxiousness.

'That will be great. A new session is soon going to begin, so we need to be quick in our decisions and considerations. Anyway, you should leave

now, or else, you'll get stuck in the traffic. Goodbye.' She smiled and waved at him.

ÞÞÞ

Manny sat with his mother at the dining table. Mummy served him an omlette with toast. Then, she carefully took out two apples from the fridge and put them into a juicer. After this, she handed the glass of juice to her son.

'Manny, do you want to go to school, like other children?'

'If you agree then why not?'

'Look dear, we-your father and I have chalked out to send you to school so that you can learn something beneficial, but seeing your sickness, I am afraid to let you go,' she said looking at her plate. A tear managed to escape out of her left eye.

'No mummy, you're perturbed for absolutely no reason. I'm fine and I'm recovering. How can I

be weak when you and daddy are my strength? I really want to go to school. Those brats who come to play in the park make fun of me, they tease me, I feel like crying then. Please permit me to go,' he pleaded.

'Are you sure?' she asked without looking at him.

'I am, mummy.'

'Alright, then be prepared for doing tonnes of homework,' mummy smiled at her little son who had just now purified all her anxieties.

TWO

'Daddy, please tie my shoelace fast otherwise, I'll miss my bus,' said the worried kiddo who was excited to attend school for the very first time.

'Done, done, but tell me, will you miss me at school?'

'Offo, daddy. I am not going to miss you at any moment there. I am a big and strong boy now. Have a look at my muscles,' the big boy said with pride.

'Anubhuti, see, our little child has grown big now,' and both, the daddy and the child bursted out in laughter.

'Here, take your lunchbox, big boy. Oh look there, your bus has arrived too.'

'Goodbye, mummy.' 'Goodbye, daddy.'

'Goodbye, son.'

Anubhuti and Vanshul kept waving until the bus reached out of sight.

'Are you still like a cat on a hot tin roof for him?'

'I am, Vanshul. Although he envelops his weakness, only we know about how strong he is, don't we?'

He sighed, 'Anubhuti, you're anxious for no reason. He'll be fine.'

ᑭᑭᑭ

'Good morning, teacher', the class wished the teacher with the typical Indian style of greeting, with the seemingly extended "d", "g" and "r".

'Good morning, everyone. Please take your seats.'

The teacher cleaned the blackboard with a duster and displayed the date neatly. Then, she went out to the school office to collect the attendance register.

'Is she our classteacher, Rahman? Is she austere?', Manny asked.

'Oh Manny, she is our new classteacher. Our previous teacher left the school after she got a better job opportunity somewhere,' answered Rahman.

'What profession can be better than teaching? This is not intelligible to me. Please elaborate.'

'You don't know. We're kids. These adults, they only go after money. We live in a society where jobs such as teaching, sweeping, etc. are not considered worthy tasks...'

'Okay, students, please respond to the attendance,' the new teacher interrupted Rahman.

'Aavi Madhya'

'Present.'

'Kashish Sharma'

'Present.'

'Sasha '

'Present.'

'Manubhav Ahuja'

'Present.'

'I think you have joined new. Come, introduce yourself.'

'Friends, I am called Manubhav Ahuja. I like playing chess..er..I've got nothing much to boast of.'

'As far as I can make out, you're too old for this class. You appear to be a boy of nine or ten years.'

'Your assumption is correct teacher. I am a boy of seven.'

'Why did you get admission in this class, then? You could have got admitted to class 2 or 5. Any exceptional cause for this?' the teacher was eager to know.

'Ma'am, I began my studies later than all of these here. I was and am sick. I am suffering from some mental disorder. Once, my psychiatrist had told me the name of this disease to my parents but, I don't remember what it is called. One and a half years ago, I used to spend

most of my time sleeping. My parents have consulted many doctors from here and there. However, they only advised me to take rest and to worry less.'

'Manubhav, you are only seven now, what stress do you have?' the teacher asked perplexed.

'I do not know, ma'am. Sometimes, when I'm asleep, I get this nightmare of the world ending and when I try to shout for help, my vocal cords do not seem to follow my command and I'm not able to utter a word. Then, the worst happens, I spot a man coming towards my bed, from my window, I try to shout for help, but again, I'm unable to speak. The man then takes out the spooky, pointed dagger that he carries with him and yells, "What will you do by being alive, when the world is coming to an end?" and subsequently, I would feel that I have regained my ability to speak and I'd shout, "Somebody save me, can somebody save me?" and after that blackout-complete blackout ma'am.'

'Then,' the teacher began, 'Why don't you sleep with your windows shut?'

'But ma'am, I don't even have a window in my room...' he murmured.

ᑭᑭᑭ

'How was my son's day at school?' Anubhuti cheerfully asked her son who had returned after the first, monotonous day at school.

'Alright but boring. Since it was the very first day, we were not taught much. It was an interaction day and I had only one boy-my partner who was kind to me, rest all made fun of me. Despite that, I'm still glad, they were not kind to me maybe because it was my first day with them. However, with time, they will befriend me.'

'Now, at this moment, I can truly believe that my little boy has finally become big now.' mummy said happily.

THREE

Spring- a season that favors growth. It's a season that gives a chance to all those who breathe to radiate liveliness. A season that is a symbol of joy and happiness.

Anubhuti was dressed up in a blue-colored salwar and was sitting on a sofa in her balcony, reading a newspaper. After a while, she got up and began watering the plants in her balcony. There were potted plants of sunflower, marigold, lily, and some typical herbs. Just then, her doorbell rang. She fled downstairs to open the entrance to her house. No one stood there. She shut the door. The bell rang again.

'Nobody' s here then, who is ringing the bell?' she thought.

The bell rang again for the fourth time, now.

'Maybe someone is at the back door. But who?' Now she got curious as well as scared.

'Vanshul is not at home. Manny is at school then, who's playing with me?'

She stood right before her door, in fright. Sweat poured down her face. She quietly opened the door and what a relief!

'VANSHUL! You are here?' she shouted.

'Yes, my lady. Is this not my home?' he said jokingly.

'It is but, why didn't you use the main entrance? I grew scared.'

'I could have but in my head, some mischief got mixed with surprise.' he laughed.

'You should have been in the office right now. What's the sole purpose of your visit, mister?' she enquired.

'It is an emergency. I have to leave for Rio Gallegos by evening so I came here to pack my files and clothes.'

Vanshul took out his trolley bag and then pulled out three big files, one of red color and the rest two reflected yellow. By the time, Anubhuti came in with three pairs of formal suits and two casual sets. She passed it to her husband and was about to say something when she heard, "Ding Dong."

She glanced at the wall clock and assumed the person on the doorstep to be Manny. She rushed downstairs.

'Welcome back home, beta.'

Manny gave her mom a quick look.

'I have a surprise for you, sweetheart.'

'What is it, mummy?' Manny asked while removing his socks.

'Wait, let me guess. Is it a watergun?'

'Come.' Anubhuti said and covered Manny's eyes with her soft hands. By the time, Vanshul came in front of him.

'What is it, mummy?' Manny asked excitedly.

'Ta da. Surprise.'

He hugged his father.

Soon, they had lunch and went upstairs to help Vanshul pack his luggage.'

'Where are you going, daddy?' Manny asked, 'To meet a zombie?'

'No, but to bring one for you.' Vanshul said and looked at Anubhuti, together, they laughed at their son's innocence.

ᑭᑭᑭ

'Anu, I'll return after two weeks. Please take proper care of Manny. Do not send him to school if he is not well and consult Aanand uncle, if necessary. Take care of yourself. Goodbye.'

'As you say, sir. You too take care. Goodbye.' she laughed.

FOUR

Vanshul Ahuja worked in the National Virus Research and Manufacture Laboratory. The scientists here were working on X-Dead 48. It was a special type of gun that could kill zombies when given proper requirements. These scientists believed that the zombies may occur in the future, but had no strong evidence to prove it. They believed that in the universe, there is a planet with the zombie population, and like us, even zombies are set on their mission to find aliens, in their terms and humans, in ours. Their latest research had found that there truly exists a virus in nature in nature that can fulfill the needs of X-Dead 48. After consulting a few linked labs, they named the virus "*CIZERA PEUTUS*". Now the question was, "Where to find, *cizera peutus* ?" Two weeks ago, their research found that the virus could be obtained from the soils of Rio Gallegos due to its cold, semi-arid climate. So now a mission was fixed and everyone selected for it had to attend it.

ꝒꝒꝒ

Vanshul took a train from Hyderabad to Chennai. There were total eight scientists sent on this mission with Gagan

Malhotra as their leading head. Three of the scientists including Vanshul were from Hyderabad and the rest including Gagan had settled themselves in Chennai. Gagan was waiting to receive them at the platform.

Since the flight to Gallegos was at night and only half a day was left and since Gagan Malhotra was a miser, he planned to truncate the expense and thus, requested each member of the mission to pass the remaining hours at a local park close by the airport.

At first, the crewmembers found it to be rather bizarre but as their hours passed with The Miser Malhotra, they understood his personality. After doing absolutely nothing than blankly looking at the children playing there, hunger knocked at the entrance of their stomachs. Everyone was hungry.

'Gagan sir, why don't we go to a café or a restaurant? I'm starving,' at last Anish managed to demand Gagan for food.

'Yes sir, we all are hungry. Please let us go to a restaurant.'

'Anish,' the miser laughed foolishly and after a few thoughts said, 'Okay, c'mon everyone, let's go to a nearby restaurant.

There was one at a distance of several meters from the park. They went into the restaurant.

'We welcome you all in Food For All,' a fat man welcomed them.

They found a table to sit at. The restaurant was neither very popular nor very busy. It mainly served south Indian food with some beverages.

'What will you all have?' asked the miser.

'I will go for a masala dosa,' Anish answered quickly.

'I'll have Hyderabadi Biryani,' Vanshul said.

And in this way, everyone placed their order except for Gagan.

He cleared his throat and said,' I wish to have a coffee.'

He smiled foolishly at Anish who was staring at him with surprise.

'Actually, I have had food before joining you all so, I'm full already.'

A waiter took their order and after 15-20 minutes served them the tasty south Indian food. The aroma of the delicious food filled the atmosphere. Everybody seemed to enjoy their order. No one said anything. Gagan felt like an idiot.

'So the food is tasty, right?' he asked stupidly.

'Yes sir,' Vanshul answered.

Gagan cleared his throat again.

'Devotion to our work is something we need in Argentina. Anyway, more on that, later.'

Nobody responded to it.

PPP

It displayed 18:00 at the airport clock. Vanshul and his colleagues had checked in at the airport. The flight was scheduled for 7 p.m. and so they had enough time left to pass. Vanshul went near to a bookstall and glanced at the books available there. Another customer came and asked the shopkeeper to give him the book he wanted.

'Which one?'

'That one.'

The shopkeeper confusingly pulled out a book and said, 'This?'

‘No, that purple cover one.’

Suddenly Vanshul caught the gaze of the book which the shopkeeper had taken out before.

‘*Bhaiya,* please give me that book. The one titled "The New World".

’Take it. 150 rupees. ‘

Vanshul returned back to his seat amongst his colleagues.

’Which book, dude?‘ Aditya asked him.

’The New World‘

’Sounds boring. I‘m reading "The Horror Of The Haunted House".

’Cool. Carry on.'

ƤƤƤ

They took their respective seats on the plane to Argentina. Vanshul had got a corner seat beside Prakash. Some passengers were still settling in. The general instructions were passed and followed. The plane took off cautiously. Vanshul began reading his book. At the airport, Aditya, the chatterbox had not allowed him to start with his book. After minutes of reading, he turned to Prakash,‘ You see, these authors are damn funny. Who expects a joke in a sci-fi book?’ but Prakash had already snoozed off.

FIVE

It was a bright Sunday morning. The potted plants, in the balcony, were in bloom. Birds were engrossed in singing their melodious song. Anubhuti with her son was sitting in her balcony.

'You have a doctor's appointment today, Manny.'

He nodded.

'Are you taking your pills timely?'

'I am.'

'Good boy. Get ready, we'll be leaving in no time.'

She then booked a taxi to take them to the clinic.

ღღღ

It was 10:45 a.m. Manny along with his mother was waiting for his turn to come. The asylum was not crowded with a handful of patients accompanied by their one or two family members but each was time-consuming. After some minutes, a lady in a nurse's fit walked to Manny and informed him that the doctor wanted their presence and so they went in.

ღღღ

'The doctor said that you're recovering,' mummy said.

'And she minimized my medicines.' Manny added,' She has done this before too. I don't think there is anything new in it.'

'There could have been but you're behaving absurdly. I think your health is deteriorating instead of improving with each passing day. Nevertheless, try your new medicines. Some miracle must occur.' She rose to gather the utensils for cleaning.

'Mummy...er...you got me wrong..listen..er,' he pleaded.

However, once mothers get angry, it is not easy to please them. His efforts resulted in vain because mummy did not listen or reply to him. He slid off his chair and walked into his room, sadly. He got onto his bed and wanted to sleep but sleep had fled with her lover, leaving Manny engrossed in thoughts. Generally, he used to doze off the moment he got onto his bed but, today was different. He was completely lost in thoughts when he discovered someone whispering near his room. The voice was familiar- yes it was his mother who was whispering.

'Err..yes..my husband is not at home and son is asleep. It's a good time for you to cast your spell on him.'

A female voice answered back,' Tomorrow, be prepared for it. He will be my prey.'

A spine ran down Manny's nerves. "Is mummy planning to kill me? Maybe yes, after all, I am only an orphan who got adopted." These thoughts of his kept haunting him and ultimately he ended up in tears.

Manny's parents were a progeny-less couple. Due to this fact, they chose to adopt a child. They had gone to an orphanage and after taking only a few steps in, a child speeded toward Anubhuti and called her, "Mummy", the best word for a lady, in the whole vocabulary. (Later, they found out that he had newly learned to pronounce that word and hence was rehearsing it every time.) A tear poured down from her right eye, she felt the happiest. She took him in her arms and it was at that moment that the seeds of love for Manny had sprouted in her heart. She had finalized that she was anyhow going to take him with her. Call it *deja vu* or the power or magic in the word "Mom", Anubhuti began to feel a strong connectivity with Manny as if he were her own son whom she must have had lost in some life. Originally, he was a child of an orphanage staff who had died while giving birth to him. Since then, he was being taken care of by other orphanage staffs.

ᑭᑭᑭ

The next day, in the afternoon, the school bell rang indicating the school dispersal. The laughter and cries of the school-going kids were enough to fill the school premises. The children rushed out from their respective classrooms in the playground. They were lined up according to their mode of transportation. The children who were allotted vans stood in one line and those who were allotted buses in the other, whereas those who lived close by were expected to form another line. Manny came in the last group.

In a while, the children who came from buses and vans had boarded their mode of transportation. 1:20 p.m. onwards, it was the time for the parents to come to collect their wards. One by one, the number of students began to decrease.

Sometime later, Anubhuti along with a strange-looking lady came to take Manny. He was puzzled as well as curious as this was his first meeting with her but he didn't utter a word.

ÞÞÞ

Soon, they were inside their house. Nobody had said anything the whole way- not even the strange lady was introduced. Neither did Anubhuti bother to introduce her guest nor did Manny ask her. The atmosphere appeared, so simple, so plain. It was only then that the bizarre woman spoke, 'Hi, people call me Manika.'

'Sorry son, I forgot to introduce her to you. This is Manika aunty, she was my school friend.' Anubhuti said and faked a smile.

'I'm Manubhav Ahuja. You can call me Manny if you like to. Nice to meet you, anyway.' Then he stared at her from head to toe.

She was dressed up in a purple-colored robe. Her fizzy, waist-length hair looked disturbing as if they were never been washed or combed in the last year. Her chapped lips parted as she spoke. Her nails had the maximum quantity of dirt which they could hold. She was a short heighted, slim, suspicious woman.

ÞÞÞ

The stars had filled the empty dark sky and were glittering like diamonds. The owl's hooting could be easily heard if one wanted to. The moon shone with all its might.

It was supper time but Manny had had already his dinner and he guessed that Manika was going to stay with them till eternity. After his mummy had consumed dinner along with Manika, he secretly asked her if it was so.

'For two more days, most probably', she replied with a smile.

He then took his pills and got onto his bed with satisfaction. He had just shut his eyes when he recalled what had happened last night, the lady to whom his mother was talking had referred to this night. He immediately sat up and decided to skip sleep that night. His mind started creating stories and questions. The most fearful and outdoing question that came to his mind was, 'Is Manika aunty the woman whose conversation he had eavesdropped on last night?' This thought began haunting him so much that he couldn't stop himself from hiding in the cupboard.

SIX

The next morning, Anubhuti couldn't find her son anywhere. She hopelessly searched everywhere for him, under the bed, beside the door, in the bathroom, in the balcony, but in vain. At first, she thought he was playing a prank on him but as minutes became hours, she sensed danger. She shared this problem with her guest, Manika who told her not to worry when she noticed Manny's slippers near the cupboard. She opened the cupboard at once, only to find Manny murmuring. Anubhuti affectionately carried him out of the cupboard and woke him up.

'Why son, why were you sleeping in the cupboard, were you afraid of something?'

Manny sprang himself out of Anubhuti's lap.

'She would have killed me, had I not hidden,' he murmured slowly.

Anubhuti ignored his statement and gave Manika a quick look.

'Look, son, everything is okay. I'm here to protect you from every evil. Have faith in me,' she told him.

He did not answer her.

After a few moments, Anubhuti and Manika left the room. They made sure that Manny wasn't around to hear them and then only Anubhuti began,' Manika, I've forced myself a lot to trust you and I hope not to get deceived by you. I think you're the only one who can help me out. Now, everything is up to you. Everything depends upon you.‘

'I won't.‘

'See, I don't dare to be around you both. I simply don't want to ruin your work with my presence, so I recommend you to execute your task in the park behind our house. Please convey everything which I've told you in the simplest language. He's only ten, he needs a special explanation to comprehend things. Be clear.‘

'Alright, I'll perform everything accordingly,' Manika assured her.

ꝑꝑꝑ

It was a bright Sunday morning. The sun was shining brightly. At times, a cold breeze would blow to make the weather appreciable. Since the park was spacious, the place couldn't be referred to as crowdy, despite the day being Sunday.

They found an empty bench under a shady tree to rest their bottoms on it.

'Aunty, have we met before?' Manny placed his first question.

'No, it's the first time,' she said and smiled.

'Why are we here and why didn't mummy come?'

'Umm.. because I want you to know me more,' she again smiled. She had very carefully ignored the other question.

'You don't want to find out more about me?'

'I already know everything about you, son.'

'What do you mean? Now you're growing scary, more due to this getup.'

'There's nothing to be scared of. You're safe with me, but,' she paused.

'But what? Oh, so we're finally on that topic. I know everything. Please spare me. Let me go, I beg you. Why do you want to kill me?' What bad have I done to you? I have had overheard your conversation with mummy when you first came to our house that night,' he pleaded.

'You know nothing, Manubhav. Absolutely nothing. Do you that your mummy is planning to kill you? Here is a spell, if you recite half of it, it will unveil the truth to you and if you speak all the lines, a protective realm will be formed around you.'

'Stop it, aunty. You have already spoken enough nonsense. It's not my mother who wants to kill me but it's you who has advised her such. My mother loves me. I also know that the moment I will speak this spell, I'll be either under your control or under death's control, so this trick of yours is not going to work on me.'

And without waiting for her reply, he left the place. On reaching home, he hugged his mother and said, 'Mummy, Manika aunty is very bad, please tell her to leave today itself,' he began weeping.

After a while, Manika walked in with her face held down in shame. When they both were alone, she told Anubhuti, 'Manny is not going to hear a single word of mine.'

'I was aware of it. Is there a spell to make things visible only to a certain person?'

'Yes, black magic can make it happen.'

'Very good. Before leaving, write the spell on a piece of paper and cast on it the spell to make things visible only to a certain person. Further, put it somewhere where Manny can easily get it,' Anubhuti told her.

'To do so, I need a nail of his. Can you tell me whether the bookshelf is an appropriate place for hiding the spell?'

'No, not the bookshelf. He barely reads. I think the mirror will be an item of elite furniture. Hide it there. He daily uses it for combing his hair before going to school.

'Alright, just arrange for his nails now.'

Sometime later, Anubhuti went into Manny's room with a nail cutter in her hand.

'Son, you know, you should follow good habits to maintain a healthy lifestyle. Check your nails, appears as if somebody has inserted grams of dust into them. You must trim them now. Take this nail cutter.

When Manny was done, his mother cautiously picked up the pieces of nails which must have settled down on the floor when he was trimming them. She then gave one of them to Manika who carried out her order.

When Manika was about to leave the house, she called out for Manny and said, 'Son, you didn't like my stay here so I'm going but what I told you was the only truth. In case you miss me someday, this mirror will carry you to me,' she gave him the antique mirror,' goodbye.'

Manny didn't answer her, he only transferred the mirror from his hand to the dining table and ran to his balcony.

SEVEN

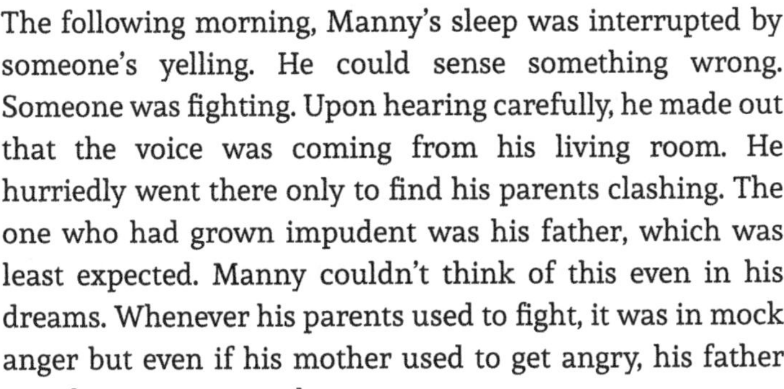

The following morning, Manny's sleep was interrupted by someone's yelling. He could sense something wrong. Someone was fighting. Upon hearing carefully, he made out that the voice was coming from his living room. He hurriedly went there only to find his parents clashing. The one who had grown impudent was his father, which was least expected. Manny couldn't think of this even in his dreams. Whenever his parents used to fight, it was in mock anger but even if his mother used to get angry, his father was the one to pursue her.

Manny stood in a corner and watched them silently, hoping that the moment they will notice him, they will stop fighting and will realize their mistake. Seven-eight minutes passed, nobody had noticed him yet. Manny couldn't even make out what his parents were fighting for. It appeared to him that they were speaking in a foreign language. Nevertheless, he waited.

A few minutes later, his father turned to pick up a hard thing, maybe a vase, and maybe to hit his wife but noticed the kid standing there. His father speeded towards him, probably to hurt him too, but Ashya got hold of Vanshul's hand and asked him to spare the little boy. Manny hurried to his room, closed his door, and sat on the floor with his legs crossed. He began thinking, 'Father was never like this.

What has happened to him now? Doesn't he love me or mummy anymore?', then he began praying,' Oh God, please cure my daddy. I cannot see him in this way. He now feels like a stranger.'

Fifteen minutes had passed when someone rang their doorbell.

'Whoever it is, he is surely going to regret ringing the bell here,' thought Manny.

The yelling stopped at once and after some silence, it turned into a peal of hearty laughter.

'Son, come her,' his father reached out for him.

'Thanks, God. I cannot believe that you have instantly granted my wish,' he thanked God in his head and ran towards his living room.

'How afraid were you!' Vanshul laughed. 'We were only playing a prank on you. Happy fool's day. You need not be afraid of us. His mother too joined them in the laughter.

Manny only smiled at them as he was busy looking at the third person who was sitting there. He wore normal, casual, summer clothes and a mask, and a pair of sunglasses. And a hat as well. He did not move.

When Vanshul found Manny engrossed in the stranger's looks, he at once said,' Son, this is the present that I've brought for you from foreign.

Manubhav looked perplexed.

'I'm your desire which you once had expressed,' the stranger said. 'I'm a zombie in plain words.'

At once, fear started flowing in Manny's veins. He moved back ten inches in fright. Pours of sweat could easily be seen on his forehead. He grew so scared that he began to shiver.

His mother went close to him to confront him. She said, 'Don't worry, dear. There's nothing to be scared of. He won't cause any harm to you as he is your father's friend.'

The little boy gathered some courage and went near him.

'Are you really a zombie? Is this another prank of yours, dad?' he questioned the two friends.

On hearing this, the stranger took off his hat and presented before him, his head, as a shred of evidence that was slit just above his forehead. Something smelly, of a bizarre color, was visible, and overall, it was disgusting. In addition to this, a poor odor had filled the atmosphere after the zombie man had taken off his cap. To show his next evidence, he took off his mask, and he had no mouth! The empty space looked awful. Heaven knows how he spoke. Next, he took off his extraordinary sunglasses only to reveal his inhuman eyes. His eyes were so popped up as if he had no hollow for eyes and someone had just glued the eyeballs on his face. His skin was rather white with faint, dark lines.

'Alright... I believe that you're a true zombie. but for God's sake, please put on your accessories back again,' the boy demanded.

'As you like it but there's no need to be scared of me. I am a friendly zombie.'

Manny applied all his efforts to put a fake smile on his face but, in vain.

He helplessly asked his father,' Where did you both meet? Dad, you were on an expedition to find some virus sort of thing then, how did all this happen? And you said that you are going to return after two weeks but, you're back before the completion of the period.'

'That is a lengthy story,' he smiled.

'Please, I request you to tell the story.'

'Alright, if you insist so much. First, let me get some juice from the kitchen,' said and walked into the kitchen.

'Had I known that zombies look this scary, I would have never wished to meet them,' thought Manny.

EIGHT

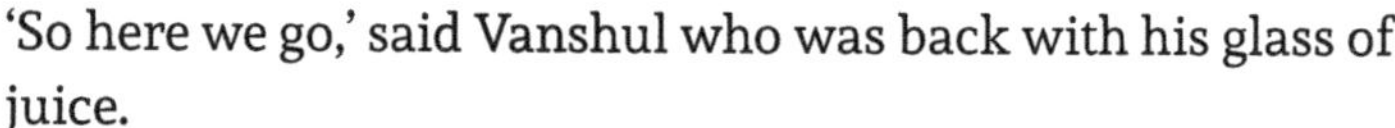

'So here we go,' said Vanshul who was back with his glass of juice.

'It is a long story, I must say,' then he cleared his throat and began,' I with eight other scientists were sent on a mission to find the *Cizera Peutus virus*- the virus which when emitted on a zombie could kill them. On reaching Rio Gallegos, the search began the next day. We tried all day long but with no benefit. After it grew dark, we speeded back towards our hotel. The following day, something unexpected happened. Gagan sir, our head in the mission was called immediately with four others who were in the mission because their previous research had provided some fruitful results. Here in Gallegos, I was made the head until their return. Now, only three scientists, including me, were left. That day we did no research. The next day, I asked my colleagues to meet me at the Silver Road Forest at 8:00 a.m. The two of those who were left with me were called Vihan and Natasha.

Honestly, I knew that Vihan was more talented than me and thus, he deserved to be the captain. Needless to say, I was also aware that the green-eyed monster must have conquered him by now, which proved correct when we got into a dispute. He was not ready to co-operate. He said that he will not follow any of my orders and that he will complain a file against my poor leadership as well. Even I got angry and cursed him. That night only, I wanted to take a train to leave that city as staying there for the whole night appeared hard to me and all the flights to India had departed that day. So, this was the only possible, immediate action that I could take. It was approximately 10:00 P.M. according to my estimation and Gallegos with its limited population had a fewer number of people to accompany me to part with my loneliness at the station.

I sat on an empty seat and looked around at the scattered population. Till where my eyes could see, there were only 10-12 people visible. I don't remember when I dozed off but, when I came back to my senses, I found somebody sitting beside me. When he figured out that I was staring at him, he said, "Hello!"

I replied, "Do we know each other?"

"We don't but, we can still be friends. You know, friendship is the journey which starts from being strangers."

"Well...I think you're right. However, I don't believe much in friends now. If today I'm leaving this city at this hour of the day, it is just because of some toxic people whom I once called my 'friends', I said.

"I believe that you first need to select people with positive and good vibes. Friendship is like a motor car that moves only with fuel. The positivity is the fuel here."

"Yeah...mhmm...true...er" I continued, "By the way, what's your name and where are you from?"

"Are we friends now?" he appeared to smile.

"Maybe" I uttered.

"I'm Pawot, not a native of this world."

"You mean you're an alien? You don't look like one."

'Aliens? Do you refer to outsiders as aliens? If it is so, then yes, I am an alien. Many get deceived by looks and pre-assumptions."

I started searching for something in my V. I.P. and then in my bag. In a few minutes, the search ended and I took out the book which I had brought at the airport. I showed it to him.

"We refer to creatures like this as aliens," I pointed at the cover page which had a picture of an alien.

He laughed hilariously, "Do I look like this? This is stupid. You, humans, are humorous. I have never seen creatures like this. On our planet, nobody roams about with such a face. Yes, but we have a scary face for, we are zombies, in normal terms.

I stood immediately and stepped back. I could hardly see 5-7 people around. When he realized that he had scared me, he began calmly, " What happened? Do you even know anything about us?"

"Yes, zombies are human-eaters. I know you want to kill us, you want to finish the human race. I know you want to establish control over this world too."

"What rubbish! It is not like that. Have you met us before? I know you haven't for, it is our first expedition to the Earth. These authors have created all false, scary stories about us when in reality, they have never seen us. Please, I request you, don't be scared of me. I shall bring you no harm."

"But how do you speak in our language? And why do you look like a human?"

"I am speaking in the same language which we use on our planet. But, I can tell you, when I was preparing for this mission, I had read in a book that there is some force operating inside us which converts foreign languages coming out from an alien's (outsider's) mouth into the general language of the person to whom he is talking to." He paused. "We don't look different from humans until the effect of a toxin/medicine vanishes and we put down our accessories.

Subsequently, he removed all his accessories, as he did today, and my face at that time was as shocked as Manny's.

"I hope this is not the makeup. In India, people play pranks on passers-by and after fooling them, apologize by saying, 'See, there's a camera hidden there.'"

"Feel my facial features, if you still doubt," he boldly said.

I had no option left but to believe him. We talked about a few more topics until the announcement for my train was made.

"I've got to go now. It was nice meeting you, Mr. Zombie," I smiled.

"Can I come along with you?" he asked slyly/shyly.

"You may but make sure not to remove your accessories. People will legit get scared if you do."

"I will follow you then. I'm, in fact, on a tour to see your world. We don't have a world like this."

In a few minutes, the local passenger train arrived at the station. We boarded it and hence he accompanied me from Gallegos to this living room.'

'Such a breathtaking story it was. I truly enjoyed it. By the way, what happened to your colleagues, daddy?' Manny asked.

'I have to leave for the laboratory this evening. My colleagues will probably arrive tomorrow or the day after tomorrow. I need to tell the higher authorities how they have made our important mission futile.' Vanshul said frowning. Then he told Manny, 'Mr. Zombie is a harmless fellow. Befriend him. He will tell you tales from his planet.'

Manny turned to the zombie and said, 'We can be friends only if you promise to tell the most fascinating tales.'

NINE

The silver sky with hues of orange, pink, and purple looked ethereal. The sun was revealing itself phase by phase. The melodious chirping of the birds reminded of the accuracy of the heavenly musical instruments. A pleasant breeze was blowing, gently touching the skin of Manny and maybe Mr. Zombie's too.

'So, you're called Manny?' asked Mr. Zombie adjusting himself on the chair kept on the terrace.

'It is my unofficial name. My full name is Manubhav Ahuja. What should I call you?'

'You must call me zombie uncle.'

'You know, even though you appear sweet, I'm scared of you...' Manny said softly.

'What other things are you scared of?' Mr. Zombie laughed.

'Of death. I get nightmares, the same nightmares on loop, sometimes, I get them while I'm awake too. My doctor says that I'm ill, I imagine pieces of stuff, but, I have a different belief. If I were to imagine things, why would my mind always create the same scenes? Almost every night, I die in my dreams. My parents along with my psychiatrist say that if I take my medicines regularly, I won't get nightmares. I do follow it seriously but I see no sign of improvement.'

'Psychiatrists are mostly mad people. They create false diseases, their causes, and earn. To stop your nightmares...'

Heaven knows what he was about to say because Manny interrupted him, not being a good listener. 'Are you scared of something?'

'My planet is a developed one. After every five years, we have a festival to celebrate our development. For that, the citizens of our world are free to go to other dormant planets, for vacation. I'm afraid of losing my way back to my planet. Our spaceships have a device installed which can trace our minds when we scan our faces in its camera. Meanwhile, we need to think of the way to reach our location and its nearby landmarks. It is a special and expensive gadget. Our brains are not mortal, we have got machines fitted instead.'

'That's interesting,' he said, 'I have heard that if zombies bite humans, we beings also become zombies.'

'If I am a good guesser, I think you have heard this from someone's mouth. If such was our strategy, why would have I waited? For an auspicious moment to come?' he laughed.

Even though he was a zombie, he had mastered humanlike emotions. Generally, zombies are expected to be dull, emotionless creatures but this fellow knew when to show what emotion.

He continued, 'We have always been blamed. We are civilized beings. We have an established world. Why would we ever kill anyone? This planet has a vast population and though we are limited, we are contented.

'I never expected myself to meet a kind zombie uncle.'
'Do you have kids?'

'No, why?'

'How do you control the population then? You must be very, very few in number.'

'We do not take birth. We are made up of some chemicals moulded together. You see this cut here, above my forehead, a machine is inserted through this slit, which you call a brain, as I stated earlier. Then, a stinky chemical is spread inside out and in the cross-section of the forehead to protect it from damages, defects, disturbances, etc.'

'That was indeed fascinating.'

'Thanks, your world is fascinating too.'

'Do you live in buildings as we do?'

'We don't. We don't have separate rooms. We live in the open air.'

'Air...do you breathe?'

'We do not function like humans, Manny. We are different from you all.'

'The air on your planet is useless if it so. You know, we have heard a lot of stories about you. About the zombie apocalypse. Have you also got stories about us?'

'We're mainly focused on our work. As I said, we are different from you humans. We hardly communicate with each other on our planet.'

'Can you create zombies from humans here?' Manny teased him.

'What for? You want me to destroy your population? I can do it if I get some chemicals from my planet and the brain of the human who is going to get transformed into a zombie. However, if even one of you gets converted into a zombie, the whole of your population will have to suffer because, the organisms produced due to the reaction of the chemicals with the human brain will spread everywhere and once they get in contact with the human body, they will bring the particular brain's doom. '

The little kid covered his gaping mouth. -----

'Who gave you information regarding all this?'

'Manny, are you going to write a book on me? Enough queries for today. Let's go down.'

TEN

The following morning was a Monday morning. Manubhav had to go to school today. Mummy, daddy, and Mr. Zombie were on the terrace. Manny had his breakfast and was all set to go to school. He came before the mirror to check his final look. Everything felt normal, except for one. The mirror wasn't reflecting Manny's appearance. He touched its surface. The same cold surface it had. He then rushed to the master bedroom. A mirror was hung on a wall opposite the window. It was the same mirror that Manika had gifted Manny four days ago. He speeded toward it to have a look and could find his reflection. He noticed a chit penetrated inside the mirror. He pulled it out. It said:

"Pulled me out to know the truth?
In the mirror, show your tooth,
It will carry you to whom?
Someone who'll save you, from your doom."

He looked in the mirror hung before him. He touched its surface and as he did it, there was a strong flash of lighting and everything around him vanished. Ultimately, he found himself in a grand room with all dimensions white. He was puzzled and was wondering about what had just happened. He thought, he was caged and felt like crying when he heard a loud sound.

"You're here because you're destined to be", it was the voice of the mirror.

A few moments later, he heard someone's footsteps approaching near him.

'Hi, nice to meet you again! I'm a magician,' a familiar voice said.

Manny looked up only to find Manika again.

'Oh, so finally, you have got me under your control? What the hell do you want from me? Let me go.' he said angrily.

'"What have I got to do with you?" That is the least important. You need to know the truth first. Before we proceed, I request you to not utter a word until I finish. If it were only for your life, I would have let it go, seeing your indifference. But when it comes to the whole of the human race, I cannot overlook it. You, only you, can protect us, by protecting yourself.'

'What I'm going to tell you is hard to believe for you. Your parents, Ashya and Virush are zombies. They are fooling you. They have drank a human potion to give themselves a fake appearance and they drink it once every three months. You are a human kid. They have adopted you to execute their nefarious plans. I don't know their plans and the sole purpose of it but it surely involves your death and all of ours too. Because you know that if one human gets converted into a zombie, all of us will also transform into them.'

'Despite being a zombie, your mother could not remain untouched by a mother's love. She told me all this, including the danger to you. She ordered me to reveal all this to you. She loves you a lot. She couldn't tell you all this for, she was afraid that you might start hating her. You can now ask me anything if you want to.'

When she turned to look at Manny, she found that tears had welled up in his eyes. It was hard for him to believe that his parents, whom he loved more than anything had such a big secret veiled.

'Crying is good, sometimes. It is all right to remove all the toxicity stored up inside you. Take your time. I'll wait.' she said.

When he was done, he said, 'If mummy loves me so much, why did she not stop all this from happening?'

'Because she can't, Manny. She can't. She will be left to decay in the space if she does so. Yet she chose to save you through me.

He sobbed. Another flush of tears was ready to take part in the truth-revealing ceremony. When the tough realization was made, he understood that it was now a null thing for him to understand why the events had gone in such a way.

He enquired Manika, 'Why did my zombie mother choose you to reveal all the secrets?'

'This was done due to two main reasons:

1) If I report this to the police, I'll be caught first.

2) Second reason, being the foremost one is, that humans have no proper weapons ready to fight against zombies. We don't know their strength, so even if the whole world attacks the two of your parents, they still have higher chances of winning.' Manika replied.

'Not only this, you must've been told that since the time you were five, you had this serious mental disorder. The fact beyond this is that your mind was and still is under the control of that stranger who came to your house, two days before.'

'I cannot do anything about it. It cannot be changed. Maybe I was destined for this. Maybe I was destined to bring a drastic change. What had to happen, has happened. As you said, if I save myself, I can save this world, can you tell me, how do I save myself?' he asked.

'It is inspiring to see a child of seven with this courage. I can see how you're holding back your tears and are trying to fight this issue. However, unfortunately, I do not have an answer to your question,' she sadly said. 'You can only find an answer to this riddle. If you recite the remaining of the magic spell, you will be saved, but only till the evening...' she began fainting.

Gradually, the dimensions vanished and he was back in his room, holding the bit of paper. He completed the remaining lines:

"*Found the truth,*
Now shivering down?
Don't worry,
She has helped you out.
Till the evening, you stand safe here,
Protected in a magic sphere."

ELEVEN

Manubhav had skipped school that Monday. A child of seven had never experienced so much stress in his entire life, till now.

"*5:30 p.m.*"

Manny lay down on his bed. The only meal which he had consumed that day, was his breakfast. A bowl of wheat barley. He knew that his hunger would only get satisfied after he finds the solution of how he could save himself and the others.

Ashya, Vanshul, and Mr. Zombie had gone missing. Heaven knows where they had found their way out of the terrace. Whether the sky ate them or the earth swallowed them. Manny was all alone in the whole house. He did not know what was going to happen next, whether he will be saved or not.

Minutes passed and summed up to an hour.

"*6:28 p.m.*"

He was still curled up in his bed, alone and shivering. Suddenly, he caught the gaze of a bottle kept on his desk. He immediately speeded towards it. 'Maybe this could help.

Zombies are decaying figures, Mummy had told me this, and, acids can burn even the hardest and the healthiest skins,' he narrowed his eyes. 'Furthermore, I don't have any other choice.

ᑭᑭᑭ

7:00 p.m.

Manny still had laid down in his bed, changing positions. He was no longer scared, he had left everything on fortune. He hadn't switched on the bulb in his room since the light was coming from the other room as the door which connected both the rooms was open.

Suddenly, someone slammed the door shut. The room had now no source of light present. The person waddled towards him. As he came close, Manny made out that it was his father.

When he was away from Manny, he said, 'I know that you have been told everything. The data in your brain justifies it.'

'Anubhuti has been successfully left in the space to decay. The chemicals which compose her body will soon shed off upon reacting with the dark energy.' there was a strange satisfaction in his voice.

'You are now of no use to us. We have wasted our time on you. We thought, through you, we will conquer this world, but, our mission has failed. Our poisonous chemicals are too mild for you all. It won't support making zombies out of you. I won't surrender, nevertheless. But since you know a lot of our secrets, you will not be spared,' he yelled.

Manny only glared at him. He felt numb. All the incidents which he had faced today were heart-wrenching and it is expected from a child of seven to react to all this vigorously.

Vanshul started coming near him. Just some moments later, he was so close to Manny that Manny could catch his breath. He said, 'What will you do by being alive when the world is coming to an end?' and subsequently took out a pointed dagger.

As he did it, Manny at once came back to his senses, it reminded him of his perpetual nightmares. Without thinking any further, he opened the bottle of acid that was resting beside him and threw the acid on him.

The zombie fell to the ground, wailing. It lasted for only a few minutes and ended with his moanings. A slimy, slippery substance was left on the floor, followed by a stinky smell.

Manubhav couldn't believe what he had done. He was getting flashbacks of the beyond-price time that he had spent with Vanshul. He numbly stood at the same place when someone approached him, calling out his name. The voice becoming louder with each passing moment. It was a familiar voice-his mother's. She was softly calling out his name 'Manubhav, Manubhav, Manny...Manubhav.'

'MANUBHAV!' she yelled.

His surroundings turned upside down when someone gave him a sudden jerk. He was more startled to find that he could open his eyes! And that he had just opened them! He had fallen asleep in the mental asylum waiting for his turn.

'So all this was only an intricate dream!' he said, inspecting his surroundings.

'It's your turn, the doctor is waiting for you. Go in. Hurry up!' the nurse said.

'What! I'm still at the clinic!' he said shockingly.

'So where do you think you should have been?' his mother enquired with a raised eyebrow.

'Nowhere. Let's go in.' he replied promptly. Now, what would he tell about what he overcame!

Author's Note

Basically, Manubhav Ahuja was suffering from a type of mental disorder called delusional disorder. He could barely differentiate between actuality and fantasy. Most of the things he said, existed only in his dreams. Hence, one could hardly say whether there was any truth in his dream, or all was a delusion.

What do you think?

Acknowledgements

To my family, for supporting me, for making me so able.

To my teachers, for guiding me.

Last yet not least, to my friends, a special mention to Aaditri, Sejal, and Supriya, for believing in me. The mention is not even half the special as you all. The world is a better place because of humans like you.

It could have never been possible without the integrated support of you all. Thanks a lot.

Printed by Libri Plureos GmbH in Hamburg,
Germany